RHYMES WOT I ROTE!

by Michael Richards

Copyright © Michael Richards 2024
Moral rights asserted.
The right of Michael Richards to be identified as
the Author of this work has been asserted by him- in
accordance with the Copyright, Design and Patents Act 1988.
All rights reserved. No part of this publication may be reproduced,
stored in a retrieval system, or transmitted, in any form, or by any
means (electronic, mechanical, photocopying, recording or otherwise)
without the prior written permission of the publisher.

*This book is dedicated to my English teacher, Mrs Russell who helped me achieve a 'D' in GCSE English literature.
Without her teachings, this book wouldn't have been possible.*

I would also like to thank Guinness, for producing such a glorious stout.

CONTENTS

HOLDING HANDS	1
THE NARCISSIST	2
14TH OF FEBRUARY	3
DOES MY BUM LOOK BIG?	4
TRIBUTE TO MY PARENTS	5
BURRITO!	6
TELECOMMUNICATIONS DEVICE	7
BROKEN WORLD	8
MY DOG	9
THE ALIENS	10
GOOGLE REVIEW	11
WORDS OF WISDOM	12-13
SWINGING!	14
QUESTIONS?	15
TURN BACK TIME	16
DIRTY SECRET	17
DISCO DANCER	18-19
THREE'S A CROWD	20
FAMILY BBQ	21
LOVE HATE	22
SOMEONE'S MADE A SMELL!	23
VICTOR	24
DEATH BY A THOUSAND CUTS	25
ALAN THE ALIEN	26-27
WORK	28
POWER & GREED	29
LOVE	30
GODS CONVOY	31
FIRST PAST THE POST	32
TOILET TIME	33
THIS IS CHRISTMAS!	34-35
NEW YEAR	36-37
THE BUNNY	38-39
THE DECEPTIVE COWBOY	40-41
THE TUBBY THIEF	42-43
DEFICIENCY	44
NEW GOVERNMENT	45
GREY PUBE	46
WRITERS BLOCK	47

HOLDING HANDS

Shall we hold hands you ask,
as we walk down the road.
Declare our love to all around,
even though we are old.

Our hands are wrinkled,
and riddled with arthritis.
I often need to use both hands,
to pick off my dermatitis.

So I don't know if we can hold hands,
like we did when we were young.
Way back then we'd also kiss,
I'd even use my tongue.

We are now old and frail,
and I find it hard to walk.
You still drive me crazy though,
oh god you don 'arf talk!

We have made it to today,
we're doing something right.
It helps that we are old,
with no energy left to fight.

So if we're going to hold hands my dear,
then please hold my left one.
As I always use my right hand,
to wipe my wrinkly bum!

The End.

THE NARCISSIST

It's hard to take my eyes of you,
such a beautiful face.
I could look at you for ages,
you make my heart race.

There's no one quite as sexy,
or as beautiful as you.
I can't see myself with anyone else,
I look forward to our next rendezvous.

I see you in the morning,
I see you when I get home.
I sometimes catch a glimpse of you,
when I'm out on a roam.

For I may be a single person,
but that doesn't bother me.
I have the beautiful you in my life,
I'm as happy as I can be.

I'm not interested in anyone else,
they don't come close to you.
You carry yourself with such grace,
I'm fixed to you like glue.

As long as I have a mirror,
or a glass to reflect my beauty.
I will remain in love with myself,
for I make myself feel fruity.

The End.

14TH OF FEBRUARY

I was born on November 16th,
and it's been pointed out to me.
Mum and dad may have done the deed,
on the 14th of February.

My brother also shares November,
as his month of birth.
Valentine's day might be the theme here,
for what that's really worth.

My parents aren't affectionate,
I've never seen them kiss.
But they must have done that dreadful deed,
for the two of us to exist.

There seems to be a pattern here,
that one day in the year.
When they both spruce themselves up,
and call each other dear.

They've clearly only done it twice,
and that's perfectly fine by me.
But as a precaution I now avoid home,
on the 14th of February.

The End.

DOES MY BUM LOOK BIG?

Does my bum look big in these trousers?
Has my face started to look old?
These are things I'm often asked,
and my thoughtful reply shall be told.

Those trousers must be faulty,
have you got the receipt take 'em back.
As for your face it's lovely,
it's the mirror that has the crack.

I have thoughtful replies for most questions,
when it comes to the good lady wife.
For if I was to answer truly,
it would only result in strife.

When my wife asks "do you love me?"
My brain doesn't have to think.
That's an easy question,
I can answer with a kiss on the cheek.

Although the wife is now older,
and has put on a couple of stone.
I'm no oil painting, yet she stuck by me,
we have love and we're not alone.

We will continue our journey together,
and it may require the odd lie.
I'd prefer that than to tell the truth,
as the truth means our love has died.

The End.

TRIBUTE TO MY PARENTS

This is a tribute to my parents,
as they've always been there for me.
I may have been the ideal child,
as an adult I owe them an apology.

I haven't been the best adult,
the best that I could be.
I've messed up in life big time,
yet my parents have stuck by me.

They could have disowned me,
try to sell me on gumtree.
Have a garage sale,
or offer me for free.

But my parents aren't stupid,
they see the trees for the woods.
They wouldn't be able to sell me,
I'd be returned as damaged goods.

So I'm really rather grateful,
to my fantastic mum and dad.
They are by far the best parents,
that I could ever have.

The End.

BURRITO!

I have a funny tummy,
it's bubbling down below.
I've eaten a hot burrito,
and I think it's about to blow!

It can't explode right now,
I have to keep it in.
I'm half way through my work shift,
the outcomes looking grim.

I have a bad feeling about this,
my face has turned a shade of grey.
My bum has begun to sweat,
it can only end one way.

I'm gonna have to make excuses,
to leave the shop floor.
The floodgates are about to open,
as I run for the toilet door.

I've managed to reach the toilet,
much to my relief.
My bum opens the cargo doors,
and releases the hot Mexican beef!

The End.

TELECOMMUNICATIONS DEVICE

My telecommunications device,
seems to have a mind of its own.
My son keeps on telling me,
it's called a mobile phone.

Doesn't matter what you call it,
it doesn't seem to work.
It keeps on changing words I type,
which makes me look a berk!

It changes 'can't' to 'can'
and 'live' it changes to 'love'
It's driving me crazy.
I've 'ducking' had enough!

I was told it would make life easier,
use to keep in touch with old friends.
I'd no longer need to use note paper,
and my trusty fountain pen.

Well those 'steeple' that told me,
have got it oh so very 'thong.'
This telecommunications device is 'salty,'
so tomorrow it will be 'John.'

The End.

BROKEN WORLD

The world appears to be broken,
there's hatred, war and greed.
I had hoped the world would progress,
and compassion and love would succeed.

It seems my hopes were wasted,
as the world has turned for the worst.
There's war in Ukraine, shortage of grain,
us citizens are being coerced.

We should be calling for better,
from the world powers that be.
That's not people like you and I,
but the ones at the top of the tree.

For they're the ones that control us,
they hold the fundamental key.
We out rule them by numbers,
but only if we all agree.

So come together for what matters,
and don't stand there alone.
Together we are mighty,
they sit there on just one throne.

The End.

MY DOG

My dog won't do a toilet,
I don't know what to do.
He walks around sniffing the ground,
he just won't do that poo!

I ask him to hurry up,
it's tiresome I'll admit.
No matter how long I wait,
he just won't do that sh*t!

I've walked around for ages,
with a poo bag in my hand.
Must be something wrong him,
it could be his anal gland?

Perhaps he needs coaxing,
maybe I can intervene?
Is there something I can do?
grease his bum with Vaseline?

I can't walk around all day,
waiting for him to poo!
He's had more than enough time,
I've important things to do!

So we head back to the car,
this mission I have had to quit.
He jumps on to the car back seat,
that's when he does his sh*t!

The End.

THE ALIENS

I don't think us humans,
evolved naturally from this place.
I believe we were created,
by an out of this world race.

They may have mixed their DNA,
with the Australopithecus.
Sat back and then waited,
the results created the Homo habilis.

Just like some experiments,
it may not have gone to plan.
So they had several goes at it,
which led to the Homo sapien.

"We've created intelligent life,
we will now keep our distance,
We'll keep a watchful eye on them,
but cannot offer any assistance."

I don't think they would be happy,
with the results of their experiment.
For the human race they created,
can only be an embarrassment.

We've shown some signs of encouragement,
to them who have been here before.
But we haven't learnt to love one another,
we have a primitive hunger for war.

They've been watching us for a while now,
have given us the benefit of doubt.
I think they know that they've created a monster,
and will be back to wipe us out!

The End.

GOOGLE REVIEW

We received a 1 star rating,
on Google review.
If you are the one who left it,
then this poem is for you!

You visited our shop today,
on the one day we have off.
That's not my problem,
you sir, can f*ck off!

You didn't receive our service,
nor a product that we sell.
But you still left a 1 star review,
you can f*cking go to hell!

I'm sorry we weren't open,
on a day we are closed.
We have personal things to do,
like shopping and washing our clothes!

Instead you could have used Google,
to check if we were around.
But instead you used Google,
to shoot our business down!

We have set trading hours,
you can't call in out of the blue.
Perhaps visit during our opening times,
when we will happily serve you.

You clearly are something special,
you have a lot of front.
Due to you leaving your 1 star review,
I think you are a c*nt!

The End.

WORDS OF WISDOM

I'd like to offer my words of wisdom,
to those much younger than me.
So you can avoid my past mistakes,
the opportunity to foresee.

So grab a pen and a note pad,
learn from my hindsight.
What I am about to tell you,
will hopefully see you all right.

Never buy white pants,
never shave your bum.
Never drink vodka straight,
never answer back your mum.

Never make a good cuppa,
never do anything for free.
Make these mistakes whilst at work,
you'll be doing them for eternity.

Don't get married before you're 30,
take time to find your true love.
Don't expect to find that person,
down at your local pub!

Never put off till tomorrow,
what you can do today.
Always avoid staying indoors,
on a lovely sunny day.

Always resolve an argument,
before you walk out the door.
You may return to find them gone,
the guilt will hurt you more.

So if you are facing life choices,
I hope you have listened to me.
Use it to your advantage,
my hindsight can be your foresee.

The End.

SWINGING!

"Let's try swinging" I ask,
you reply with a moan.
I want to try swinging,
and can't do it alone.

"It might be good fun,
can't we let ourselves free?"
By the look you wear upon your face,
you totally disagree.

Our life has got rather boring,
perhaps it could do with a lift?
It could be that swinging,
may stop our relationship drift?

So why don't we try swinging?
It might be really fun.
The very last time I had a swung,
it was with my mum!

I still remember today,
way back when I was young.
My mother took me to the park,
the swing was so much fun!

I don't know why you disagree,
when I suggest swinging to you.
I can push you and you can push me,
it might be a fun thing to do?

The End.

QUESTIONS?

Did man land on the moon?
is the earth really round?
If a tree falls down in an empty forest,
does it make a sound?

Were the pyramids made by humans?
Did the city of Atlantis exist?
Did Lord Admiral Nelson,
really ask Hardy for a kiss?

If you don't sleep for 3 days,
can you go out of your mind?
Is there a pot of gold at the end of a rainbow?
For I never seem to find.

Is it possible to love,
without feeling pain?
Can you live on junk food,
without any weight gain?

Loads of daft questions,
occupy my inquisitive mind.
How many times can you touch yourself,
before you go blind?

The End.

TURN BACK TIME

These are things I wish I had done,
but back then I didn't know.
If I was able to turn back the clock,
I'd give them a jolly good go!

I wish that I had the confidence,
to be able to get up and dance,
I wish I had learned to skateboard,
but I didn't get that chance.

I would have liked to asked Brenda,
out to the school ball.
I'd liked to have told Ruben,
his knitted shorts were really cool.

I wish I had gone travelling,
seen the world's wonderful sights.
Alas, that didn't happen,
due to my dreadful fear of heights.

I can turn back the clock in October,
but only by one hour!
I need a clock that can turn back years,
I need Harry's magical power!

The End.

DIRTY SECRET

I love the way you look,
I love your beautiful smile.
You conduct yourself with such grace,
you make living life worthwhile.

I love to run my fingers through,
your beautiful thick dark hair.
I love to stroke your lovely face,
it's the perfect love affair!

You are so incredibly intelligent,
you know about a lot of things.
When you debate with others,
you run them around in rings.

You are so damn perfect,
in every single way.
Don't listen to the idle gossip,
suggesting you are gay!

The love we hold for each other,
could be considered the ultimate sin.
We wouldn't want to upset others,
we'll keep our love held in.

I will keep our dirty secret,
I know that you will too.
As long as I have a travel mirror,
I will always be with you!

The End.

DISCO DANCER

He was the greatest disco dancer,
that Bolton had ever seen.
He moved like no other,
he had limbs like plasticine.

Everyone would stand and watch,
when he graced the dance floor.
His dancing would leave you breathless,
he'd leave you wanting more!

He'd drive the ladies wild,
with his rhythm and thrusting hips.
He moved like no other,
he was heading to the championships!

However, it all ended rather badly,
for this Bolton disco dancer.
You ask me the question why?
I'm about to give you the answer.

He'd been working on a move,
that hadn't been seen before,
He'd practiced it numerous times,
but only behind closed doors.

The move required going commando,
wearing pants would be restricting.
It was to be his downfall,
and horrendous for those witnessing.

His routine so far had gone as planned,
time to execute his special move.
It was the championship final,
and he had a lot to prove.

His left leg went up in the air,
his upper body gracefully reclined.
His right arm pointed up,
his left hand grabbed his behind.

He thrust his body upwards,
committed to a somersault.
His trousers couldn't take the thrust,
too late for him to abort!

The seams of his trousers gave way,
and exposed his crown jewels.
Aunt Brenda had a heart attack,
disqualified for breaking the rules!

The End.

THREE'S A CROWD

Brought up to recognise partnership,
as couples, in units of two.
My mindset has since been changed,
as she seems to know what to do.

This is not your average person,
that has got me in the sack.
She's taken control of the situation,
I'm commanded to get on my back.

She's riding me like a Yamaha,
my asthma is making me wheeze.
She's told me to get on all fours,
carpet burns upon my knees!

I'm feeling rather saucy,
shown things I've not seen before.
When suddenly I hear another voice,
followed by a knock on the bedroom door.

"Who the hell is that?" I ask,
"I thought it was just you and me?"
Turns out that she has a husband,
they like to do things in threes!

The introduction of her husband,
put me right off my stride.
I kept looking over my shoulder,
keeping an eye on my backside.

Well we've heard three is a crowd,
and I'm grateful that rung true.
Thank god that he doesn't like to partake,
he just likes to take in the view.

The End.

FAMILY BBQ

The sun is out and I'm feeling great,
it's time for us to have fun.
We'll get the old barbecue out,
let's invite everyone.

We have chicken and burgers,
and sesame seeded buns.
Plenty of booze to drink,
even Guinness for my mum.

Our families will come together,
on this lovely sunny day.
They will mingle with each other,
in their own unique way.

There will be uncle Eric,
arguing with his latest wife.
My dad will be telling stories,
about his adventurous life.

My nephew will be fixated,
upon your aunty's breasts.
He will be wearing sunglasses,
to hide his gaze from our guests.

Helen will drink too much,
throw up on her boyfriend Derek.
This day has been so much fun,
it's left me in hysterics.

It's been a lovely day,
spending time with family and friends.
They may be a messed up bunch,
but it's sad when it has to end.

The End.

LOVE HATE

You like to make my life miserable,
with your unkind words.
You put me down and insult me,
yet I've put up with it, it's absurd.

You say I'm not capable of love,
which I know isn't true.
I regularly experience the feeling of love,
as I love to hate you.

You like to say that I'm cold,
you are welcome to your view.
But I'm warm to those who I like,
it just happens that I don't like you.

You like to point out my faults,
I could point out your faults too.
For once I'll tell you my actual thoughts,
I'm thinking of divorcing you.

The End.

SOMEONE'S MADE A SMELL!

Someone's made a smell,
can only be one out of three.
There's four of us in our living room,
and it certainly wasn't me.

Could it have been my dad?
for his wind is renowned,
His bottom is rather weighty,
but it would've surely made a sound?

So that leaves just two others,
that could've let that fart go.
It is either mum or my brother,
I now have got to know.

The smell is rather bad,
it has an accompanying fog.
This smell shouldn't be in our living room,
it should be safely down the bog.

I think it might have been my brother,
his face wears a gleeful smirk.
I think I saw him lift his bum cheek,
did he set off that dud firework?

It might have been my mum,
as she got up to make tea.
She was conveniently in the kitchen,
by the time the smell reached me.

Well I never got to the bottom,
of which bottom made that smell.
Time ran out and the smell dispersed,
the culprit was saved by the bell!

The End.

VICTOR

I've been told that I'm miserable,
and that I always like to moan.
Apparently if you talk to me,
you'll end up emitting a groan.

I never intend to bring others down,
with the things that I have to say.
If you see me before I see you,
you'd be wise to walk away.

Should you get my attention,
I will stop and talk to you.
You'll soon realise you made a mistake,
you'd have more fun in bed with the flu!

The End.

DEATH BY A THOUSAND CUTS

'Death by a thousand cuts',
is one of my favourite figures of speech.
Alas, I feel that's become a reality,
freedom may soon be out of our reach.

What about 'divide and conquer,'
that's a powerful phrase.
The policy of maintaining control,
separate us so we can't liaise.

The 1% got nervous,
it looked like the 99% could unite.
They weren't going to lose control,
so divide us up and watch us fight.

The battle looks like it's been lost,
the righteous cannot win.
We the 99% were daft,
we fell for the 1% spin.

The End.

ALAN THE ALIEN

Greetings my name is Alan,
I'm an alien from out of space.
I've travelled many light years,
to visit the human race.

There are many different races,
in this vast universe.
But none quite as special,
as what you have on earth.

It is our duty to visit planets,
that has life with intelligence.
Help them on the right path,
if we witness signs of negligence.

Humans have the ability,
to evolve and achieve great things.
You need to learn to love one another,
before transformation can begin.

This is my advice to humanity,
accept you are all the same.
Appearance doesn't matter,
empathy, compassion should be your aim.

It doesn't matter if you're different,
whether by abilities, size or skin.
As beauty is not found on the outside,
true beauty is found within.

So treat each other kindly,
never be unkind.
Hate is taught to those who listen,
consuming is a waste of your mind.

You humans stand a chance,
come together as one race.
For the sake of protecting humanity,
stop the fighting and embrace.

Your planet is rather special,
humanity needs to pull through.
Earth and it's life must be protected,
with or without you!

The End.

WORK

I can't get out of here,
this place I call work.
It always keeps me captive,
it drives me berserk.

I start the day with optimism,
but once the clock strikes four.
Optimism grabs his coat,
and walks out of works door.

I wish I was like optimism,
and had the balls to get up and leave.
I still have work left to do,
for me there's no reprieve.

The End.

POWER & GREED

Why is the world unkind,
there's bullying, killing and war.
Have we as humans not learnt,
from the history we've seen before?

Humanity is controlled by them,
those who are racketeers.
Power and greed are their motives,
they've done it for hundreds of years.

I think a change is needed,
for the human race to succeed.
Don't cancel words of Roald Dahl,
but the words 'power' and 'greed'.

'Power' and 'greed' has got us here,
humanity should reassess.
Perhaps if we were to cancel those words,
the world wouldn't be in a mess?

The End.

LOVE

Use the word love sparingly,
you don't want to wear it out.
If you use that word often,
the meaning will have less clout.

It's an intense feeling of deep affection,
and should be reserved to demonstrate that.
It shouldn't be freely thrown around,
used in day to day chit chat.

You might love fish and chips,
you might love watching football.
You might love Tom Cruise,
you'd be forgiven, don't we all?

Consider switching love for like,
to protect the words intent.
Use love when only heart felt,
in the way the word was meant.

The End.

GODS CONVOY

I've got to give up my vices,
the ones that I really enjoy.
Life's journey is getting shorter,
I'm riding in God's convoy.

So the cigarettes have got to go,
the beer, women and rock 'n' roll too.
The crack pipe needs to go back in it's box,
that leaves me with not much to do.

I don't have any hobbies,
my vices were all that I had.
But if I carry on as I have been,
I'll end up a dead beat dad.

So I have to give up my vices,
if I still want to be around.
See my daughter grow up,
keep those I love safe and sound.

God's convoy doesn't stop,
the time keeps on ticking.
My vices will only shorten my life,
it's time for me to get quitting!

The End.

FIRST PAST THE POST

I am in the political wilderness,
there is no party that represents me.
First past the post no longer works,
P.R. is where we should be.

There are only two main parties,
that only ever stand a chance.
Both appear to be lacking ideas,
to them it's a song and a dance.

Career politicians are useless,
our concerns they won't engage.
Not content to serve us the people,
they seek only the world stage.

They look to create drama,
conflict is a glorious thing.
A chance for them to write memoirs,
further their career and coin it in.

We now have a sitting government,
playing out the end game.
They aren't going to do good things,
for the next government to claim.

Time to change our political system,
so that it represents us all.
End the childish board game,
that is played by the Etonian faithful.

The End.

TOILET TIME

I've sat down on the toilet,
to do a number two.
Watching TikTok while I wait,
what else is there to do?

I give a gentle push,
to help it on its way.
It's putting up such a fight,
I think it wants to stay.

I rock from side to side,
trying and shake it loose.
It doesn't appear to be working,
time for cranberry juice?

I won't give up that easily,
I'm committed to see this through.
I've managed to get its head out,
maybe it will like the view?

It's clearly rather stubborn,
it's hanging on within.
Perhaps it has anxiety issues,
perhaps it's unable to swim?

Well I can't stay here all night,
trying to coax it out.
I have other things to do,
I'll have to call time out!

The End.

THIS IS CHRISTMAS!

For f*ck sake it's December,
the last month of the year.
It is the time for giving,
get sloshed on wine and beer.

For this is Christmas,
the time when I will pretend.
Pretend to be happy and joyful,
can't wait for Christmas to end.

My Stanley wants a PlayStation,
my Sarah wants a new boyfriend.
Fiona, my wife wants a divorce,
the wanting never ends.

For this is Christmas,
it's that time of the year.
People wanting for presents,
sure to cost us all dear.

Her parents will come over,
her sister, husband and kids too.
They will takeover our house,
like a South American coup.

For this is Christmas,
it's that time of the year.
The family get together,
we'll all be insincere.

I don't feel this is Christmas,
how it is meant to be.
It's lost its true meaning,
that's now clear to me.

For this should be Christmas,
a time of the year.
To share love and kindness,
to those we hold dear.

So let it be Christmas,
doesn't need a spending spree.
Just share love and kindness,
we can do that for free.

The End.

NEW YEAR

Here comes the new year,
you want me to resolve.
Change my undesirable traits,
accomplish our goals.

I've listened to what you've said,
perhaps I should change my ways?
Have I become blind sighted,
whilst wandering in life's big maze.

You want me to do what's right,
you say it will be good for us.
You want me to discard my vices,
calmly without any fuss.

You've listed so many vices,
I was thinking it would be just one?
You say it's better to address them all,
and then the job is done.

Smoking is top of the list,
alcohol is number two.
You say that these are valid asks,
I'm inclined to agree with you.

Number three is a problem though,
you want me to give up my friends?
This isn't your average new year resolution,
it's a hate list that never ends.

A new year resolution,
should be kept nice and simple.
You'll want to stay focused,
It needs to be achievable.

So, I've made my own resolution,
my vices live on another year.
It's time for me to visit a solicitor,
you can shove your list my dear!

The End.

THE BUNNY

I see a little bunny,
running up the hill.
Running through the daffodils,
on a mission to fulfil?

Why is that bunny running?
is he running away or to?
Perhaps meeting a lady bunny,
and is late to his rendezvous?

I see the farmer running,
running up the hill.
Shouting explicits as he goes,
on a mission to fulfil?

Why is that farmer running?
is he running away or to?
Perhaps he's after that bunny,
he wants him for a stew?

I see the farmer coming back,
running down that hill.
Calling out for assistance,
his mission not fulfilled?

He's quickly followed by the bunny,
who appears to have had enough.
The bunny's standing his ground,
he called the farmer's bluff.

That little bunny's brave decision,
caught the farmer unprepared.
The bunny's bluff had paid off,
had the farmer running scared.

Should you ever feel hounded,
asked to do something you don't want to do.
Stand your ground like bunny did,
the bluff may work for you.

The End.

THE DECEPTIVE COWBOY

He was 4 foot 10,
way back then in 1865.
Unless you knew how to handle yourself,
it was hard to stay alive.

It was the wild wild west,
a lawless place for such a little man.
He'd reached 20 years of age,
he now needed a master plan.

He drew 10 warning posters,
hung them around his town.
The posters stated he was dangerous,
not to be messed around.

He would walk into the saloon,
people would stop and stare.
They'd heard he was dangerous,
they got up and went elsewhere.

All was fine for a while,
till a marshall arrived in town.
He saw the danger posters,
was his duty to take him down.

The marshall called him out,
time for him to come in.
The little man had to act fast,
in order to save his skin.

"I've done nothing wrong sir,
although a moral sin.
I've told a white lie to survive,
In order to save my skin."

The sheriff listened intensely,
to the story he was told.
He realised this kid had brains,
perhaps he should be enrolled?

This is a story about deception,
brain is mightier than brawn.
What we see and are told,
we happily accept and move on.

So question what you read,
or what you happen to see.
Those that put it out there,
may just want you to believe?

The End.

THE TUBBY THIEF

There were four pairs of socks on the washing line,
now there's only two?
Where the hell the other two pairs went,
I haven't got a clue.

This isn't the first time it's happened,
last week it was my mum's bra.
I've got to get to the bottom of this,
next week it could be the car?

It seems that we have a thief,
that's stealing our washed clothes.
I set up cameras in the garden,
surely the thief will be exposed?

My dad's vest was the next to go,
it must have been caught on tape?
Playback confirmed my suspicions,
witnessed the thief making his escape.

For the thief was a tubby squirrel,
seen him in the garden before.
Now I knew who the perpetrator was,
I decided to investigate some more.

So off I went to fetch a ladder,
lent it against the big ash tree.
Climbed up to the thief's house,
to see what I could see.

The tubby squirrel was fast asleep,
using my sock as a sleeping bag.
Mum's bra was a swinging hammock,
Dad's vest had become a beanbag.

All that squirrel was missing,
was a nice flat screen tv.
Maybe that was the next item,
he was planning to steal from me?

The End.

DEFICIENCY

My mood has considerably changed,
I've developed tits and a beer belly too.
I feel so incredibly tired,
the working day is hard to get through.

I find it difficult to concentrate,
on the tasks I have today.
Forgetfulness is another symptom,
I've forgotten what I wish to say.

I know that I have to do something important,
that requires my professional view.
But Brenda's decided to eat an apple,
all I can hear is her munch and chew.

My concentration is being disturbed,
my energy levels are very low.
I used to like those that I work with,
but today I've told them where to go.

F*ck off Brenda with your apple,
and Todd you can f*ck off too!
I've woken up with titties and a belly,
no sympathy from either of you.

The tits are fun to play with though,
when I am at home alone.
I've since visited the doctors,
I'm lacking in testosterone.

The End.

NEW GOVERNMENT

They're coming for the working class,
they're coming for you if you smoke!
They've only been in power 8 weeks,
already this government's a joke.

They're coming for the pensioners,
the winter fuel allowance now gone.
Yet the left will remain quiet,
Sir Starmer can do no wrong!

They're coming for business owners,
the unions are now in control.
Their demands will be granted,
which the rest of us will bankroll.

They're coming for freedom of speech,
they don't want you to disagree.
For as long as you remain silent,
then you will still be free.

They're coming for your inheritance,
they'll say it's for the greater good.
They don't care about your parents wishes,
they'll take it like Robin Hood.

They don't want to discuss,
topics that we want addressed.
They'll mess around with what already works,
leave our country in a mess.

Inflation will go through the roof,
taxes will rise too.
Maybe it's not your problem?
It will be when they come for you!

The End.

GREY PUBE

I've found a grey pube,
I'm in despair.
Me bits down there,
are the same as me hair!

So what should I do?
Do I try back to black?
Apply to me balls,
by rubbing on me sack?

Hang on a sec,
there are side affects.
My current lovely balls,
could get proper wrecked.

So I ask me dad,
if he's had the same thing.
He sat me down,
and began to sing...

"Son, don't you worry about the little grey hair.
There will soon be many that you just won't care.
That little grey hair is neither here nor there.
You should be worrying about...

...the cost of living!"

The End.

WRITERS BLOCK

I've dried up like a raisin,
I have nothing left to write.
I've sat with my pen in hand waiting,
but my mind has no appetite.

My brain was once active,
I'd always have something to say.
My mind is now distracted,
on getting through the day.

Life has got much harder,
harder than it once was.
I think it's finally taken it's toll,
my brain has now switched off.

Perhaps it's time to move on,
my brain doesn't want me to write.
Time to turn the lights off,
time to say goodnight.

x

The End.

Thank you for reading.

Printed in Great Britain
by Amazon